GOOD MORNING!

Prayers for Children
from Around the World

Berkley Books by Wayne Lee Jones

WEAVE A GARMENT OF BRIGHTNESS
GOD, GOOD MORNING!

GOD,
GOOD MORNING!

Prayers for Children
from Around the World

Wayne Lee Jones

BERKLEY BOOKS, NEW YORK

This book is an original publication of The Berkley Publishing Group.

GOD, GOOD MORNING!

A Berkley Book / published by arrangement with
the author

PRINTING HISTORY
Berkley trade paperback edition / September 1997

The Putnam Berkley World Wide Web site address is http://www.berkley.com

ISBN: 0-425-15980-9

BERKLEY®
Berkley Books are published by The Berkley Publishing Group,
200 Madison Avenue, New York, New York 10016, a member of Penguin
Putnam Inc.
BERKLEY and the "B" design
are trademarks belonging to Berkley Publishing Corporation.

PRINTED IN THE UNITED STATES OF AMERICA

10 9 8 7 6 5 4 3 2 1

This book is dedicated to my parents,
LaRue Lee and Janet Marion Jones,
who taught me how to live life
as though it were a prayer.

Introduction

While doing the research for another of my anthologies, *Weave a Garment of Brightness,* I came across a number of beautiful prayers for children that I felt deserved attention but did not fit the plan of that work. Thus I began to collect children's prayers exclusively, an effort that resulted in this volume. During the process of assembling these prayers, I rapidly discovered that most of the anthologies of children's prayers currently available suffered from a lamentable lack of respect for the religious experiences of children, emphasizing rhyme and rhythm over content. These collections, while perhaps providing a satisfactory source of songs and poems for very young children, did not answer the needs of maturing children for sound content and provocative imagery.

A useful anthology of children's prayers that answered

the rapidly changing needs of children seemed necessary. The selections in this volume are arranged in an order of gradually ascending complexity, both in language and in content. This does not mean they must be used consecutively. In sharing these prayers with their children, parents will discover the prayers that meet their particular needs. Furthermore, because each child is unique in his or her spiritual development, the prayers have not been grouped in sharply divided age levels. Some younger children may be able to grasp the more complex prayers, while some older children may favor the sound and repetition that feature prominently in the earlier prayers.

The prayers in this volume are collected from numerous sources, from many cultures and religions around the world. I have composed a few myself, inspired by the materials I encountered. In many cases, I have retranslated or paraphrased prayers to conform language to modern standards and clarify contents. In these instances, the meanings and structures of the prayers have been preserved as closely as possible.

In many cultures, there are no distinctions made between prayers for adults and prayers for children. Children learn the devotions of the community by continual exposure to them, enjoying first the sound and shape of the words themselves, then absorbing, through the context in which they are presented, an understanding of their meaning and function. In reading these prayers, bear in mind that not all of them were written with children specifically in mind, but that children would be exposed to them and recite them along with adults.

It is hoped that parents will use the prayers in this anthology with their children. Children look to their parents as spiritual models. When parents pray, children will pray. Parents may also use this anthology as a source of ideas for creating their own devotions, for themselves and for their children. The sincerest form of prayer is that which emerges spontaneously, from inside oneself.

Perhaps the most significant lesson to be learned from this collection, for children and their parents, is that despite their religious and ideological differences, human beings have the same spiritual wants and needs. Though the prayers in this anthology come from many different cultures and many different authors, they offer a single picture of the human longing for God. Both children and adults experience this longing. When we appreciate it in one another, we are opened to a common humanity that transcends doctrinal or political differences.

A Note to the Young Reader

This book is full of beautiful prayers, words that people from all over the world use to talk with God. I put this book together hoping that these prayers would become yours, too. They show many different ways to pray to God, and there are many ways you can use them. They can be read quietly, by yourself, or shared with parents or friends, or made into songs. Even if saying just one line or just one word feels right to you, that one line or one word can be a prayer all by itself.

I also hope that this book will encourage you to make up your own prayers. All over the world, people tell their secrets and their needs and their dreams to God, and I think that no matter what words people use, God hears them. Remember that the most wonderful part of praying is just saying the prayers. No matter how or when or why, when we use our voices and hearts and minds to pray to God, we make the world around us even more beautiful.

I hope you enjoy this book and that it shows you that

God, Good Morning!

the prayers of other people are no different from your own. Although we may be different or come from different places, in our hearts we are all very much alike and God hears us all.

GOD,
GOOD MORNING!

Prayers for Children
from Around the World

Praying's easy.
Every morning,
first of all, I say,
"Good morning, God!"
and then
I talk to Him all day.
He's never
very far away.

Helen Caswell

Lord, I can run and jump and shout and SING!
I can skip and clap and stamp and SWING!
Thank you for making me alive!

Sister Frances Claire of St. Saviour's Priory

Bless everyone I love, God.
And bless me, too. Amen.

Mary Manz Simon

We thank thee, O God, that we are able to gather
with our friends.

A traditional blessing from Indonesia

I see the moon,
And the moon sees me;
God bless the moon,
And God bless me.

A traditional American prayer

Thank you, God, for this new day
In my school to work and play.
Please be with me all day long,
In every story, game and song.
May all the happy things we do
Make you, our Father, happy, too.

Anonymous

Dear Father, bless this day,
And bless me, too;
Bless me in all I say,
And all I do.

Elfrida Vipont

Dear God,
bless the people
who wipe away my tears
when I cry!
They hug me
and make me feel happy
again.

Lois Walfrid Johnson

God bless all those I love;
God bless all those that love me;
God bless all those that love those that I love;
And all those that love those that love me.

From an old New England sampler

God made the sun
And God made the tree,
God made the mountains
And God made me.

I thank you, O God,
For the sun and the tree,
For making the mountains
And for making me.

A traditional American prayer

God, You put the light in morning.
God, You put the dark in night.
God, You gave me all my senses:
Taste, touch, smell, hearing and sight.

God, You made the whole world for me
A place to grow and work and play.
God, please help my life be pleasing
As I enjoy every new day.

Wayne Jones

Make me, dear Lord, polite and kind
To every one, I pray.
And may I ask You how You find
Yourself, dear Lord, to-day?

John Banister Tabb

When I pray I speak to God, when I listen God
    speaks to me.
I am now in his presence.
He is very near to me.

Anonymous

Dear God,
Bless us all and keep us safe.
Thank you for all you have given us
and all the goodness we shall receive.
Bless our family and friends.
Keep us safe.
And forever will my soul be with you.

Kelly Jones

May everyone be happy!
May everyone,
weak or strong,
thin, fat, or in between,
short, small, or very tall,
people we see and people we don't see,
people who live near us and people who live far
    away,
people who have been born and people who will be
    born in the future,
may everyone,
with no exceptions,
be happy!

A prayer of the Buddha recorded in the Suttanipata

O Father of goodness,
We thank you each one
For happiness, healthiness,
Friendship and fun,
For good things we think of
And good things we do,
And all that is beautiful,
Loving and true.

Anonymous

Thank you for loving
all the little children
in the world
the way you love me.
Show me how to be a good friend
to others
now
and when I am grown up.

Lois Walfrid Johnson

God, please help me use my body
the way it should be used.
My eyes are for seeing the good all around.
My ears are for listening to beautiful sounds.
My feet are for walking all over the ground.
My hands are for helping the friends I have found.
Thank you, God, for making my body.

Wayne Jones

As we meet together here

May we have joy in learning,
joy in using our hands,
joy in listening,
joy in singing,
joy in seeing lovely things,
joy in thinking together.

Here let the hours be bright
with work and play and friendship.

A song of the Student Christian Movement

Little drops of water,
little grains of sand,
make the mighty ocean,
and the pleasant land.

Little deeds of kindness,
little words of love,
Help to make earth happy,
like the heaven above.

A traditional English prayer

Thank you for the sun,
the sky,
for all the things that like to fly,
the shining rain that turns grass green,
the earth we know—
the world unseen—
for stars and night, and once again
the every morning sun. Amen.

Myra Cohn Livingston

God,
You made the world so
everything has a place.
Fish have a place:
they live in the water.
Birds have a place:
they fly in the sky.
Plants have a place:
they grow in the ground.
I have a place
with my family.

Wayne Jones

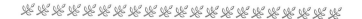

All things bright and beautiful,
All creatures, great and small,
All things wise and wonderful,
The Lord God made them all.

Each little flower that opens,
Each little bird that sings,
He made their glowing colors,
He made their tiny wings.

The tall trees in the greenwood,
The meadows where we play,
The rushes by the water
We gather every day—

He gave us eyes to see them,
And lips that we might tell
How great is God Almighty,
Who has made all things well.

Cecil Frances Alexander

O God who created and loves all creatures
I think of the animals that must work so hard,
the oxen that have to pull heavy burdens,
and the donkeys that carry big loads.

Care for the hungry donkeys
and make people kind to animals.

A folk prayer of India

Dear Father, hear and bless
Thy beasts and singing birds
And guard with tenderness
Small things that have no words.

A traditional English prayer

Oh, the Lord is good to me,
And so I thank the Lord,
For giving me the things I need:
The sun, the rain, and the appleseed;
The Lord is good to me.

A prayer of John Chapman, known in American folklore as
Johnny Appleseed

Please give me what I ask, dear Lord,
If you'd be glad about it,
But if you think it's not for me,
Please help me do without it.

A traditional American prayer

Dear God,
Be good to me:
The sea is so wide
And my boat is so small.

The prayer of a Breton fisherman

Sweet Mother, stay by my side.
Gaze upon me;
Come with me everywhere
So that I am not alone.

A prayer to the Virgin Mary from Mexico

Help me remember that You love me.
Help me remember that You are near.
Help me remember that You made me.
Help me remember there is nothing to fear.

Wayne Jones

Wherever I go—only You!
Wherever I stand—only You!
Just You!
Again You!
Always You!
You, You, You!
When things are good—You!
When things are bad—You!
You! You! You!

A Hasidic song

Thank you for time to play and time to work,
time to think and time to dream.

Juliet Harmer

God's the only One who knows
the thoughts we're thinking
in our minds.
I read good books
and think good thoughts
so He'll be pleased
with what He finds.

Helen Caswell

Day by day, dear Lord,
Of Thee three things I pray—
To see Thee more clearly,
To love Thee more dearly,
Follow Thee more nearly,
Day by day.

Richard of Chichester

Lord of the loving heart,
May mine be loving too.
Lord of the gentle hands,
May mine be gentle too.
Lord of the willing feet,
May mine be willing too.
So may I grow more like thee
In all I say and do.

Phyllis Garlick

I ask God please
to guide my hand
with anything I have to do,
so what I make is beautiful
and maybe useful,
too.

Helen Caswell

My God, I offer you
All the thoughts,
Words and deeds of this day.
I ask you to bless me, my God,
And to make me good today.

A traditional prayer from Mexico

Sometimes, God,
my friends need me.
Sometimes I can be
of help to them.
Remind me, God,
to listen closely.
Show me how I can be
of help.

Wayne Jones

Let us always remember
to be kind to one another.
If we are loving and caring
we shall always have friends,
and if we have friends,
we shall never be sad for long.

Juliet Harmer

Be with the people
who are sick and sad and hungry.
Show me how to share with them.
Help me so I don't waste anything
you have given me.

Lois Walfrid Johnson

Oh Thou great Chief,
light a candle in my heart,
that I may see what is therein,
and sweep the rubbish from Thy dwelling-place.

The prayer of an African schoolgirl

Lord, thou knowest how busy I must be this day.
If I forget thee, do not thou forget me.

Sir Jacob Astley

Forgive us, God, for the bad things we have said and
    done.
Help us to be kind again to one another instead.
Give us your spirit so that we may live happily
    together in this beautiful world you have given
    us.
And please make people in every land love their
    enemies as well as their friends.

Anonymous

Look! Our Mother Earth is lying here.
Look! She gives us good food to eat.
She gives us her power.
Let us thank Mother Earth, who lies here.

Look! Our Mother Earth is covered with growing
    fields.
Look! She fulfills her promise to feed us.
She gives us her power.
Let us thank Mother Earth, who lies here.

Look! Our Mother Earth is covered with
    spreading trees.
Look! She fulfills her promise to feed us.
She gives us her power.
Let us thank Mother Earth, who lies here.

Look! Our Mother Earth is crossed by running
    streams!
Look! She fulfills her promise to feed us.
She gives us her power.
Let us thank Mother Earth, who lies here.

*From the Hako ceremony of the Pawnee tribe of
Native Americans*

This is a song to the whole world.
This is a song to the beauty of the sun and the
      moon.
This is a song to teach young children.
This is a drinking song sung by old men.

Let us laugh and be happy in the world that belongs
      to our King.
Let us sing and dance in His kingdom.

A folk song of Mongolia

Give me, O God, your blessing
Before I give myself to sleep;
And while I slumber
Watch over all those I love.

For my mother, for my father,
For my brothers, I pray
That you keep them long years
In health, strength, and happiness.

Give solace to the sad,
And health to the sick,
And bread to the needy,
And to the orphan, protection and a roof.

We all worship you
For all that we owe you.
And as we sleep our last sleep,
We shall awaken in your bosom.

A traditional prayer of Colombia said before going to sleep

Eternal God,
Thank you for waking me from my sleep.

Eternal God,
Thank you for letting me see
The beauty you have created.

A prayer recited upon arising by Kelly Jones

Happy are they who tell the truth,
For their words are believed.
Happy are the helpful,
For they know that they are needed.
Happy are they who make things,
For they have gifts for others.
Happy are they who play fair,
For they are welcome in games.
Happy are the friendly.
For they make friends.

Doris Clore DeMaree

If I am angry or annoyed,
may I think before I speak.
If I have to defend myself,
may I keep my head, and do nothing cruel.
May I be ready to protect another
against bullying or hurtful teasing.
If someone has done wrong to me,
may I be ready to forgive,
and to be friends again.

Anonymous

We love our God
And sing his praises every day
Who has made the Sun and the Moon,
And sprinkled twinkling stars in the sky.
We love our God
Who has created this universe with oceans,
      mountains, and rivers,
Who has made beautiful flowers bloom,
And bountiful trees bear sweet fruit.
We love our God
Who has taught sweet songs to the birds and
      melodious humming to the honeybee,
Who is the giver of wisdom, knowledge, and
      strength,
And the beacon light to show us the right path.
We love our God
Who showers his love and blessings on children and
      makes them intelligent and good.

A traditional prayer of India

Blessed are You, Lord, our God,
King of the World,
Who has things like these
in His world.

A Jewish blessing recited upon seeing beautiful people or natural objects

O God, bless all the people for whom life is hard
    and difficult:

Those who are ill and who must lie in bed at home
    or in hospital;

Those who cannot walk or run or jump and play
    games;

Those who are lonely because they are away from
    home;

Those who are sad because someone they loved has
    died;

Those who are not very clever and for whom it is a
    struggle to keep up with the rest of the class;

Those who are shy and who find it difficult to meet
    people;

Those who are poor and never have enough.

Help me, O God, to remember all such people, and
    to do all I can to help them.

William Barclay

Open our eyes
for your truth.

Open our eyes
for your will.

Open our hearts
for your love.

Open our hearts
for your joy.

Open our hands
for your work.

Open our hands
for one another.

From the Lutheran World Federation

Where is your house, God,
You who give life?
I am looking for you.

O You who give life,
Your house is in every place.
Princes ask for your help
upon a blanket made of flowers.

In the place where the drums play,
every kind of tree flowers.
You are in that place.

From a poem by the Aztec poet Aquiauhtzin

O God!
You are peace
and the fountain of peace.
Our Lord,
allow us to enter Paradise,
the house of peace.
You are blessed,
Lord of Majesty and Honor.

From the Muslim daily prayer

O God, you have let us pass the day in peace,
Let us pass the night in peace.
O Lord, you have no Lord,
There is no strength but in you.
There is no unity but in your house.
Under your hand we pass the night.
You are our mother and our father.
You are our home.
Amen.

A prayer recited before going to sleep from the Iona Community of Scotland

I give thanks to You, O King, living and eternal,
because You have put my soul
back inside me, with kindness—
Your faithfulness is very great!

A Jewish prayer recited upon arising

For all that has been—Thanks!
To all that shall be—Yes!

Dag Hammarskjöld

God, I want to thank You
for my parents,
even though they don't always make me happy,
and for my friends,
even though they don't always do what I want to do,
and for my school,
even though it's not always fun,
and for the world I live in,
even though there are things I don't like in it.

God, sometimes You give me things I don't want,
but I know they are there because You want them
    to be.
God, let me want the things that You want,
so I can be happy with the things I have.

Wayne Jones

God be in my head,
And in my understanding;
God be in my eyes,
And in my looking;
God be in my mouth,
And in my speaking;
God be in my heart,
And in my thinking;
God be at my end,
And at my departing.

From the Sarum Primer, published in 1558

As the daylight follows night,
As the stars and moon give light,
So dear Lord, with all your might,
Care for me.

As the Springtime brings the flowers,
As the minutes turn to hours,
So, dear Lord, with all your powers,
Care for me.

As with Peace the swift-winged Dove,
Looks upon me from above,
So, dear Father, with thy love,
Care for me.

Olwen Godwin

Over there, over there!
See the fair rainbow,
See the rainbow brightly clothed and painted!
Now the swallow brings good news to our corn,
Singing, O Come here, come here,
Come here, rain, come here! O
Singing, O Come here, come here,
Come here, white cloud, come here! O
Now we hear the corn plants whisper,
O We are growing everywhere! O
Hi, yai, the world is fair!

From a corn grinding song of the Native Americans of the Southwestern
United States

Water, you are what brings us life.
Let us find what we need to drink so that we may
    be happy.
Let us drink the delicious drink you bring,
as though you were the mother who loved us.
Let us go to the house of someone you have
    brought life,
and let us be reborn.
Let the spirits help us for our benefit,
and let us have water to drink.
Let the spirits pour health and benefit over us.
Water, please take away everything bad inside me,
everything that I have lied about,
and whatever bad thing I have decided to do.
Agni, full of water, come and let happiness wash
    over me.

*From the Rig Veda 10:9, an important collection of religious hymns
of the Hindus*

You are blessed, Lord, our God,
King of the Universe,
You remember Your promise,
You can be trusted when You make a promise,
and You are faithful to Your word.

A Jewish blessing recited upon seeing a rainbow

O Lord Almighty,
Lord of mountains and trees,
Lord of lightening Spring
And beautiful Autumn,
Lord of pity and mercy,
We worship thee.

Lord of mercy,
Lord of multicolor clouds
And the East and the West
And the blue sea and the golden sun,
We worship thee.

O Lord Almighty,
Lord of waters, winds and storms,
We worship thee.

A traditional prayer from Lebanon

Our Father which art in heaven,
Hallowed be Thy name.
Thy kingdom come.
Thy will be done, as in heaven,
So in earth.
Give us day by day our daily bread.
And forgive us our sins;
For we also forgive every one that is indebted to us.
And lead us not into temptation;
But deliver us from evil.

The Lord's Prayer, from the Gospel of Luke 11:2–4

❀❀❀❀❀❀❀❀❀❀❀❀❀❀❀❀❀❀❀❀

God!
Fly through your house
Walk about in the heavens
And go into the house of the spirits.

The heavens will obey you
They will be closed
The heavens will tremble
They will be thrown down to the ground.

A religious song from the Solomon Islands, praising God for His power to
create thunder and rain

O Pusan, travel the roads, and keep away fears.
God, stay with us, and go in front of us.
O Pusan, chase away the wolf who frightens us,
and chase away the robber who waits for us.
Guide us safely from those who pursue us,
and make our journey easy and glad.
Guide us to fields with lush, green grass,
and keep us safe from sickness.
O Pusan, help us find understanding.

*From the Rig Veda 1:42, an important collection of religious hymns
of the Hindus*

Keep me safe!
Keep me safe!
Tonight belongs to the gods.
Watch over me, God.
Stay close to me, God.
Keep me safe from magic spells
from dying in my sleep
from doing what is wrong
from talking badly about others
and from others talking badly about me
from schemes
and from fights over property.
Let us have peace, my God!
Keep me safe from the fierce warrior
who makes us afraid,
whose hair stands up!
May my spirit and I rest peacefully tonight,
O my God.

A Tahitian family prayer

Greetings to the Holy Law!
It was the good of the ancient times.
It was the good of the middle times.
It is the good of the present times.
It makes good sense.
It has good words.
It is a pure Law.
It is perfect and opens our minds.
It is a pure Law.
It is very clear.
It has no confusion.
It lasts forever.
It shows the right way.
It satisfies everyone's desires.
It benefits those who are wise.

A Tibetan Buddhist praise of the religious law

And you will love the Lord,
your God,
with all of your heart,
with all of your spirit,
and with all of your strength.
And let these words,
which I command you today,
be upon your heart.
Teach them to your children,
speak of them when you sit in your house
and when you go on your way,
when you lie down
and when you arise.
Bind them as a sign on your hand
and let them be symbols between your eyes,
and write them on the doorposts of your house
and on your gates.

*A prayer from the Jewish daily liturgy rehearsing some of the ritual
obligations of Judaism*

Love the inward, new creation,
Love the glory that it brings;
Love to lay a good foundation
In the line of outward things.
Love a life of true devotion,
Love your lead in outward care,
Love to see all hands in motion,
Love to take your equal share.

Love to love what is beloved,
Love to hate what is abhorr'd;
Love all earnest souls that covet
Lovely love and its reward.
Love repays the lovely lover,
And in lovely ranks above,
Lovely love shall live forever,
Loving lovely loved love.

A hymn of the Shakers

We bring our praise
for all swift motion:
the blowing wind,
and rippling, flowing water;
the flying birds,
and planes that follow
the airways above us;
the moving of fish in the stream;
the power of motion in our limbs:
the power to run and leap
and dance and swim.
For all swift motion
and for our joy in it
we bring our praise.

Edith Kent Battle

In the name of God,
the Compassionate,
the Merciful.

May God,
the Kind,
the All-Seeing,
give peace to everyone,
big and small.

God is more powerful than all of them
put together.

Peace!

From the prayers of the Sufi saint Abu Sa'id ibn Abu al-Khayr

Today I am your child.
Today I am your grandchild.
What I ask you, you will do.
What you ask me, I will do.
You will take care of me.
You will stand up for me.
You will lift your hand to protect me.
You will speak up to protect me.
May nothing that comes from streams under trees
    hurt me.
May nothing that comes from under plants hurt me.
May no blowing winds hurt me.
May no falling rains hurt me.
May no flashing lightning hurt me.
May dew still wet the ground for me.
May pollen still come from the plants for me.
May the way before me be pleasant.
May the way behind me be pleasant.
May I live a long time.
May I be happy.
It has become pleasant again.
It has become pleasant again.

A prayer from the Navajo tribe of Native Americans asking for protection
    from harm

O God!
Forgive me,
my father and my mother,
my teachers and my companions,
the believing men and the believing women,
the Muslim men and the Muslim women,
for You are the Most Merciful
of all those who show mercy.

From the Muslim daily prayer

Most Blessed One!
You have always been absorbed
in peaceful meditation.
You fill us with wonder.

Blessed Lord!
We ask that you make our confusion
disappear.
We ask that we may find enlightenment
in this life.
We ask that when we are born again
we may come back to this world
to help others.

Blessed Lord!
We devote our lives to helping others,
in thanks to our Lord Buddha.

A Buddhist prayer from the Surangama Sutra

We thank You!
Every soul and every heart rises up to You,
Whose name is pure,
Whom we give honor when we say "God,"
and whom we praise when we say "Father,"
for the kindness
and tenderness
and affection of a father
come to all of us from You.

We are happy
because we have been filled with the light of Your
knowledge.
We are happy
because You have shown Yourself to us.

A prayer used by Hermetic communities in the Mediterranean region
around the second century

Here, in our world,
the One Who Gives Life paints with flowers,
flowers with colors like the feathers
of the quetzal bird, in Spring.
This is how our Father acts;
maybe He acts this way in His own house.
The priests, wearing necklaces of red feathers,
dance over the land,
in the place where the beautiful drums are heard,
in the place where the beautiful flutes are heard,
the instruments of the beautiful God,
Lord of the heavens.

From a poem by the Aztec poet Cacamatzin

You are blessed, Lord, our God,
King of the World,
Who by His word brings the evening,
opens gates with wisdom,
changes periods with understanding,
turns the seasons,
and arranges the stars as He wills
in their constellations.
He creates day and night,
moving light before darkness
and darkness before light,
dividing between day and night,
the Lord, Lord of Hosts, is His name.

A Jewish prayer recited in the evening

Each day the first day:
Each day a life.

Dag Hammarskjöld

What is the Teaching of the Buddhas?
It is not to do evil.
It is to do what is good.
It is to cleanse your mind.
This is the Teaching of the Buddhas.

What is the Teaching of the Buddhas?
It is saying only good things.
It is doing no harm.
It is keeping yourself away from what isn't good.
It is eating only what you need, and not too much.
It is living in a peaceful home.
It is trying to think clearer thoughts.
This is the Teaching of the Buddhas.

From the Buddhist text known as the Dhammapada

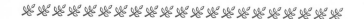

I believe in the sun even when it does not shine.
I believe in love even when I do not feel it.
I believe in God even when he is silent.

A Jewish prayer found on a cellar wall in Cologne, Germany

Let us give honor to the one who is full of prayers
who does not meditate
who does not say the religious services
but, without any effort,
reaches the glory of Shiva.

Though I am young, when I taste Your service,
I am wise, like someone with gray hair.
The happiness You give is forever attached to You;
May Your service be forever attached to me.

A Hindu song in praise of Shiva

Lord,

God of those who came before us,

Who made heaven and earth and all the beautiful
    things in them,

Who gave shores to the sea by Your command,

everything shakes in fear before You,

and none can stand beneath Your anger,

but the mercies that You promised never end.

For You are the Lord,

patient and merciful, with great compassion,

feeling sad over the evil things that people do.

Lord, Your grace is sweet.

You have promised forgiveness to those who right
the wrongs they have done.

I will always praise You,

through all the days of my life.

The hosts of heaven praise You,

and sing to You forever.

From "The Prayer of Manasseh," composed around the second century B.C.

O Lord, this solemn prayer comes from deep desire:
May my life be as pure as candle fire.

Let my every breath dispel the world's gloom,
Let my spirit glow so brightly that darkness meets
    its doom.

May my life enhance my country's glory
As the flower enhances the garden's splendid revelry.

May I be as faithfully drawn to learning
As the moth is drawn to the candle's burning.

May my life be devoted to serving the needy
And to loving a sorrowful, ever-suffering humanity.

Lead me away from the path of temptation.
O Lord, let truth alone be my destination.

A traditional prayer of Pakistan

God,
I cannot talk to you
as I talk to my friends.
You do not answer me
in a voice I can hear.
Yet you are the God Who hears prayer.

I cannot see you
as I can see the world around me.
You are not seen in one shape
or in one place.
Yet you are the God Who sees everything.

God, teach me what it means
for you to hear
for you to see
so that my own hearing
and my own seeing
may be clearer.

Wayne Jones

The sun is the happiness of those
who wait for it to rise;
my happiness is the Lord.

He is my sun
and His rays have given me life;
His light has driven the darkness from my face.

I found my eyes in Him,
and saw His holy day.

I found my ears in Him,
and heard His holy truth.

Hallelujah.

*From the "Fifteenth Ode of Solomon," a pseudepigraphical work dated to the
second century*

God,
You are God because You choose to be,
You are the only one who can give Yourself thanks.
When we try to know who You are, we can come
        very close to You,
But You are always different from what we think
        You are.

From the Munajat of the Sufi saint Abdullah Ansari of Herat

You are blessed, Lord, our God,
King of the World,
Who forms light and creates darkness,
makes peace and creates everything.
He is the One who gives light to the earth
and everything that lives on it, with compassion,
and in goodness makes new with each day, always,
the work of Creation.
How great is Your work, Lord!
You have made everything with wisdom,
filled the world with Your possessions.
Lord, may You be blessed,
over the praises of Your work
and over the bright lights that You have made,
may they glorify You!

A Jewish prayer recited in the morning

Lord, shining rays of light have shone
from the sun of Your grace.
They have made the petals of the lotus of my heart
    open,
so that it breathed out the sweet scent of
    Knowledge.
I am always grateful to You for it;
I worship You always in meditation.

Bless me in everything I do,
so that I may bring good to others.

From the Hymns of Milarepa, the devotions of a legendary master of
Tibetan Buddhism

God made this universe from love
For Him to be the Father of.
There cannot be
Another such as He.

What duty more exquisite is
Than loving with a love like His?
A better task
No one could ever ask.

Rahman Baba, a seventeenth-century Pathan poet

It is glory enough for me
That I should be Your servant.
It is grace enough for me
That You should be my Lord.

An Arabian folk prayer

In the name of God, the Beneficent, the Merciful.
Praise is God's, Lord of the worlds,
the Beneficent, the Merciful,
King of the Day of Judgment!
It is You that we worship, and it is You we beg for
     help.
May You guide us on the straight path,
The path of those You have favored,
not of those who have made You angry,
nor of those who have gone astray.

The opening chapter of the Koran, recited in the Muslim daily prayers

As the rain hides the stars,
As the autumn mist hides the hills,
As the clouds veil the blue of the sky,
So the dark happenings of my lot
Hide the shining of thy face from me.
Yet, if I may hold thy hand in the darkness,
It is enough,
Since I know that,
Though I may stumble in my going,
Thou dost not fall.

A Scottish Gaelic prayer

I said to my mother,
"Who is this God, who is supposed to be
      everywhere,
Yet is not in our house?
You tell me there is none kinder than he.
You say he is never separated from his creatures.
Why don't I at least see him in my dreams?
Why doesn't he answer my prayers?
I see thee at thy devotions every morning;
Yet I haven't seen him."

My mother answered me gently.
"Seek him in thine own heart.
He is in the color and the fragrance of the flowers.
The spring garden and the blossoms are evidence of
      his Being.
God is in chastity and in goodness.
He can be seen in the rays of the sun.
Trust in God in everything you do, my son,
And do not offend your fellowmen
by any act of unkindness."

A prayer from Iran

God,
You made a world
where not everything is easy.
You made a world
where we can't always tell
right from wrong
beautiful from ugly
good from bad.
Help me to see the two sides
of everything.
Help me to choose the side in everything
that you want me to choose.

Wayne Jones

There is something bigger than everything.
It fills the whole universe.
It has been always.
It will be always.
It is the mother of all things.
I do not know what it is called, so I call it
Tao.

Tao is greater than heaven.
Tao is greater than earth.
Tao is greater than rulers.
Tao is greater than every other great thing.

From the Tao Teh Ching

We know that food is God,
because living things are made from food.
They live by food when born,
and enter into food when they die.

We know that breath is God,
because living things are made from breath.
They live by breath when they are born,
and enter into breath when they die.

We know that mind is God,
because living things are made from mind.
They live by mind when they are born,
and enter into mind when they die.

We know that understanding is God,
because living things are made from understanding.
They live by understanding when they are born,
and enter into understanding when they die.

We know that joy is God,
because living things are made from joy.
They live by joy when they are born,
and enter into joy when they die.

From the Taittiriyaka Upanishad, a sacred book of the Hindus

May I walk with beauty in front of me.
May I walk with beauty behind me.
May I walk with beauty above me.
May I walk with beauty below me.
May I walk with beauty all around me.
May I walk as someone with happiness and a long
    life.
It is finished in beauty.
It is finished in beauty.

The ritual formula that ends most prayers of the Navajo tribe of
Native Americans

Index of
First Lines

God, Good Morning!

God, Good Morning!

God, Good Morning!

God, Good Morning!

You are blessed, Lord, our God, King of the World, Who
by His word, 80
You are blessed, Lord, our God, King of the World, Who
forms light, 90

Acknowledgments

Pages 1, 33, 36: From *A Little Book of Prayer* by Helen Caswell. Nashville: Thomas Nelson, Inc., copyright © 1995. Reprinted by permission of Thomas Nelson, Inc.

Page 3: From *God's Children Pray* by Mary Manz Simon. Copyright © 1989 Concordia Publishing House. Used with permission.

Pages 4, 29, 37, 46, 50, 65, 86, 96: Copyright © William I. Kaufman, *The UNICEF Book of Children's Prayers;* originally published by Stackpole Books, 1970. Reprinted by permission.

Page 7: "Bless This Day" from *Bless This Day: A Book of Prayer for Children* by Elfrida Vipont, copyright © 1958 by Harcourt Brace & Company and renewed 1986 by Elfrida Vipont, reprinted by permission of the publisher.

Pages 8, 17, 40: Copyright © Lois Walfrid Johnson. *Hello, God!* Minneapolis: Augsburg Publishing House, 1975.

God, Good Morning!